58oi 4589

Dear Parents and Educators,

Welcome to Penguin Young Readers! As parents and educators, you know that each child develops at his or her own pace—in terms of speech, critical thinking, and, of course, reading. Penguin Young Readers recognizes this fact. As a result, each Penguin Young Readers book is assigned a traditional easy-to-read level (1–4) as well as a Guided Reading Level (A–P). Both of these systems will help you choose the right book for your child. Please refer to the back of each book for specific leveling information. Penguin Young Readers features esteemed authors and illustrators, stories about favorite characters, fascinating nonfiction, and more!

The Princess and the Pea

LEVEL **2**

GUIDED
READING **H**
LEVEL

This book is perfect for a **Progressing Reader** who:
- can figure out unknown words by using picture and context clues;
- can recognize beginning, middle, and ending sounds;
- can make and confirm predictions about what will happen in the text; and
- can distinguish between fiction and nonfiction.

Here are some **activities** you can do during and after reading this book:
- Read the Pictures: Use the pictures in this book to tell the story. Have the child go through the book, retelling the story just by looking at the pictures.
- Making Inferences: In this story, the queen uses a pea to test if the princess is real or not. What do you think the queen is looking for in a real princess? What do you think makes a real princess?

Remember, sharing the love of reading with a child is the best gift you can give!

—Bonnie Bader, EdM
  Penguin Young Readers program

*Penguin Young Readers are leveled by independent reviewers applying the standards developed by Irene Fountas and Gay Su Pinnell in *Matching Books to Readers: Using Leveled Books in Guided Reading*, Heinemann, 1999.

Penguin Young Readers
Published by the Penguin Group
Penguin Group (USA) Inc., 375 Hudson Street, New York, New York 10014, USA
Penguin Group (Canada), 90 Eglinton Avenue East, Suite 700, Toronto, Ontario M4P 2Y3, Canada
(a division of Pearson Penguin Canada Inc.)
Penguin Books Ltd, 80 Strand, London WC2R 0RL, England
Penguin Ireland, 25 St Stephen's Green, Dublin 2, Ireland (a division of Penguin Books Ltd)
Penguin Group (Australia), 707 Collins Street, Melbourne, Victoria 3008, Australia
(a division of Pearson Australia Group Pty Ltd)
Penguin Books India Pvt Ltd, 11 Community Centre, Panchsheel Park, New Delhi—110 017, India
Penguin Group (NZ), 67 Apollo Drive, Rosedale, Auckland 0632, New Zealand
(a division of Pearson New Zealand Ltd)
Penguin Books, Rosebank Office Park, 181 Jan Smuts Avenue, Parktown North 2193, South Africa
Penguin China, B7 Jaiming Center, 27 East Third Ring Road North,
Chaoyang District, Beijing 100020, China

Penguin Books Ltd, Registered Offices: 80 Strand, London WC2R 0RL, England

Text copyright © 1996 by Harriet Ziefert. Illustrations copyright © 1996 by Emily Bolam. All rights
reserved. First published in 1996 by Viking and Puffin Books, imprints of Penguin Group (USA) Inc.
Published in 2013 by Penguin Young Readers, an imprint of Penguin Group (USA) Inc.,
345 Hudson Street, New York, New York 10014. Manufactured in China.

The Library of Congress has cataloged the Viking edition under the following Control Number: 9539341

ISBN 978-0-14-038083-5   10 9 8 7 6 5 4

ALWAYS LEARNING   PEARSON

The Princess
and the Pea

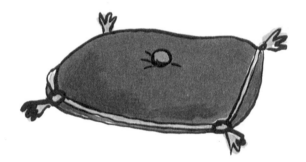

retold by Harriet Ziefert
illustrated by Emily Bolam

Penguin Young Readers
An Imprint of Penguin Group (USA) Inc.

There once was a prince,

who wanted to marry a princess.

But she had to be a *real* princess.

The prince looked and looked.

He met many princesses.

Many, many princesses!

Many, many, many princesses!

But the prince sent
all of them away.
He did not think they
were *real* princesses.

One day there was a big storm.

A princess knocked at the door.

"Come in," said the king.

"Come in," said the queen.

11

Oh, what a drippy
princess!

Her hair was drippy!

Her dress was
drippy!

Her shoes were

drippy!

12

But still she said

she was a *real* princess.

The queen said, "I will see.

I will see if this is a *real* princess."

And off she went to make the bed.

15

First the queen

put a tiny pea

under the mattress.

Next, the queen put

1 . . . 2 . . . 3 . . . 4 . . . 5 . . .

6 . . . 7 . . . 8 . . . 9 . . . 10 . . .

mattresses on top of the pea.

Then she put

1 . . . 2 . . . 3 . . . 4 . . . 5 . . .

6 . . . 7 . . . 8 . . . 9 . . . 10 more

mattresses on top of them.

On top of the twenty mattresses,

the queen put twenty down covers.

Then she called the princess.

"Your bed is ready!" she said.

The princess went to bed.

Oh, what a sleepy princess!

In the morning the queen asked,

"How did you sleep?"

And the king asked,

"How did you sleep?"

And the prince asked,

"How did you sleep?"

"I did not sleep," said the princess.

"I did not sleep at all!

I did not sleep because there

was a big lump in my bed."

The king and queen smiled.

"You must be a *real*
princess!" they said.
"Only a *real* princess could
feel a pea under twenty
mattresses!"

The prince married the princess, because he knew she was a *real* princess!

And the pea?

They saved it for ever and ever.